PINOLE

I0393929

For Primmy Bunny

Little Bunny

Biddle Bunny

paintings & verse by David Kirk

SCHOLASTIC PRESS

CALLAWAY

NEW YORK

Little bunny, Biddle bunny
Squeezed in Mommy's nest.

Ears and noses, tails and toeses,
How can bunny rest?

Does the big, wide world outside
Smell wonderful and new?

Do the pretty flowers sway
As if to call to you?

Little bunny, Biddle bunny
Time for you to go

Find a million small delights
A bunny ought to know!

Friends to play with,

Treats to eat,

Sunny meadows, warm and sweet.

Such a big, brave Biddle bunny
Out and on your own.

Are you happy, little one?

Or do you feel alone?

Little bunny, Biddle bunny
Warm in Mommy's nest.

Ears and noses, tails and toeses,
Help a bunny rest.

Nicholas Callaway, Editorial Director
Antoinette White, Senior Editor • Sarina Vetterli, Assistant Publisher
George Gould, Production Director • Toshiya Masuda, Designer
Carol Hinz, Editorial Assistant • Laurie Feigenbaum, Contracts Director
Ivan Wong, Jr. and José Rodríguez, Design and Production Associates
With thanks to Jennifer Braunstein at Scholastic Press and to Raphael Shea, Art Assistant, at David Kirk's studio.

Library of Congress catalog card number: 2001 131878

ISBN 0-439-33819-0

10 9 8 7 6 5 4 3 2 1   02 03 04 05 06

Printed in the U.S.A.
First edition, February 2002

The paintings in this book are oils on paper.

THIS BIDDLE BOOK BELONGS TO